Gossamer Ghosts

A Story from an Unusual Apocalypse

Robert J. McCarter

Little Hummingbird Publishing

Foreword

This story was originally published in 2022 in *Pulphouse Fiction Magazine Issue #18.*

Other titles in the world of Gossamer:

- *Gossamer Threads*

Contents

Gossamer Ghosts

I CAN REMEMBER THE moment when I knew that we were screwed. All of us. The entire human race.

And that's something.

It was after eight p.m. on a cold February night and I stood behind the bar, my feet aching from having been standing so long and being too damn old to tend bar anymore. CNN was playing above me, a near constant since the aliens arrived. The Treaty was being signed and CNN had their main line anchors on covering it, the coverage oscillating between the talking heads, live footage of the signing taking place at the United Nations headquarters in New York City in the vast assembly hall, and more live footage from the protests outside the building.

The bar was long and narrow with brick walls and short windows high on the wall, a basement space recently built out below a historic hotel in Flagstaff, Arizona. This was my bar, well mine and my partner's and the bank, of course.

The crowd was heavy for a Wednesday and not just college kids, but all ages. No one wanted to be alone for this.

It was a little warm from all the bodies and smelled sharply of fear, but there wasn't that much talking, most of it low whispers.

This wasn't like a Sunday when football was playing or like a weekend when the college kids came out looking for companionship. This wasn't our usual sleepy Wednesday night. This was it. Right here. The defining moment of our generation and everyone knew it.

"Gossamers will do us in," a local man said, nodding to the screen. That was what some people called them. Gossamers. It's because it was how they looked, how their ships looked, all glisteny and silver as if lit by an inner light. "Goodbye freedom," he continued. "Goodbye America."

The aliens were in the elegant assembly hall, three of them, tall and thin and looking like they were made out of moonlight. They were humanoid with long graceful fingers and large expressive eyes. They wore long gossamer gowns and I could not tell their gender much less tell them apart.

We didn't know much about the aliens, even little things like if they had gender.

I nodded at the man and wiped the bar in front of the fool. I didn't believe him, but my job was strictly apolitical. "Another beer?" I asked.

He nodded, not looking at me, his tired eyes narrowing as he stared at the screen. He was dressed in a flannel shirt and jeans, at a bit over forty, just about my age, with short brown hair slipping to gray.

It was like he was my doppelgänger except the look on my tired face was one of hope, not fear.

His stare was so intense, so filled with hate, that I turned and looked. Parked in front of the aggressively rectangular UN building was one of their spaceships. It looked similar to the reflective bean sculpture they have in Chicago, but smaller and without the hump, its silvery surface more than just reflective, glowing. It showed the crowd of screaming protesters with their signs and their hate, the group of counter protesters with their different signs and different hate, and the line of police dressed in riot gear keeping them all back. There were piles of dirty snow and everyone was bundled against the code, their breath coming out in clouds.

The ship was a symbol and it said something different to either side.

To many it said hope for a brighter future, one with less violence and better medicine, one where they would help us reverse the effects of climate change, one where the world had no nukes and war was a rarity, not a constant.

To others, it was giving up what was essential about them, one where we were subject to an authority higher than ourselves, one where religion looked foolish and antiquated, one where the world was not our own anymore. This was the first step of a hostile invasion to them and it was to be fought. At any cost.

Because of the local who looked a lot like me, I saw it happen live. I saw the puffs of smoke. I saw the pavement under the ship crumble and I saw it fall. And then I saw the explosion that gutted forth and flashed out briefly, flames licking the tall UN building while the camera shook and then went black.

There were gasps in the bar and then everything went silent.

They had tried it before, those that saw this as the end. They had tried hurting the alien ships, but it had always failed, their technology seemingly impervious to their efforts and the kinds of explosives the other side had been able to muster.

The screen was blank for a good five seconds that felt like at least five hours before it popped back to the panel of talking head. The silver-haired moderator had his hand to his ear and said, "We...we are not sure what just happened. An explosion of some sort. I am being told that there is extensive damage and casualties. And...the aliens have disappeared. We'll be right back with details after this commercial break."

That was the moment.

I knew we were screwed.

It felt like a gut punch, like it was personal, like it was serious. I wanted to throw up and run away and hit somebody all at the same time.

If the aliens had wanted to destroy us, they could have easily, but they came to help, and we just blew up one of their ships.

We were so screwed.

———

THE NEXT DAY I called my ex to check on her. We hadn't talked in at least six months, but I knew Tracy well enough to know that this had hit her hard.

I was pacing the hardwood floor in my small house south of Flagstaff a bit, coffee buzzing through my veins and the scent of it filling the house. My living room faced the forest and I could look out and pretend that I was alone.

Which might be a strange thing for a lonely guy to do. Move to a small community outside a small city, make friends, but not any really good ones, have a very social job but hide from the world when you aren't working.

Except Tracy, I didn't want to hide from Tracy. I didn't want to be divorced from Tracy or estranged from our daughter, Grace, but there it was.

My living room was simple. Big brown couch, big flat screen TV on the wall across from the couch, coffee table, bookshelves, all very neat.

The phone rang, for a long time, and when it picked up, I heard coughing.

"Trace? Are you okay?" I asked. "It's me. It's Glenn."

She cleared her throat loudly. "I know it's you, Glenn," she said, her voice sounding tired. "You are on my contacts list."

I felt stupid and my cheeks flushed red and I was glad she couldn't see it. Tracy was always good at that. It's not like I didn't know how cell phones worked. I hadn't been tending bar all my life, I had been an HR executive down in Phoenix. The bar and Flagstaff were my escape. "Are you okay?" I asked, ignoring the jab and asking my question again.

"I'm fine," she said with a sigh. "What do you want, Glenn?"

Except she didn't sound fine. Not at all. Her voice was phlegmy and she sounded exhausted.

"The thing...the Treaty," I began. She had me off-center. She was still mad at me for our "irreconcilable differences." Which to me didn't amount to much more than me being way overworked and being an introvert who withdrew to recover. "I just thought that...you know... It's a terrible thing. I wanted to check on you."

"I'm fine," she repeated. She didn't ask me how I was doing. It had been long enough since the divorce that she was usually at least civil.

Something was going on but it was clear she wasn't going to tell me.

"I was just checking on you," I said, trying to sound cheerful. "Seeing if you wanted to talk about it."

She sighed again. "Thanks for calling, Glenn. I've got to go."

I sat down on my couch and popped open the laptop and went to Facebook. I can't stand the site, everyone either pretending their lives are fabulous or fighting with each other. I made sure Grace hadn't unfriended me yet—she hadn't, that was a relief—and sent her a quick message: "What's up with Mom? Is she okay?"

It didn't take long. I knew Facebook wasn't her preferred social app but it was the one I actually understood and I knew she lived on her phone. And I had hoped that the topic of her mother would get her to communicate.

"She's got cancer. Pancreatic. Bad." I stared at the screen.

"What can I do to help?" I typed back. "Nothing," was the instant reply.

———

ABOUT SIX MONTHS LATER, I was working at the bar on a Wednesday night. It was Fourth of July and people were kind of losing their shit. At least the ones that were glad the aliens left.

That attack at the UN did destroy one of their spaceships, killing the aliens on board as well as killing a few hundred protesters and doing serious damage to the UN building.

Manhattan has tunnels all over the place. The authorities haven't released many details, but the Patriots—that's what they call themselves—used existing tunnels and extended them under the circular plaza in front of the UN building.

They had planned this. For a long time. They had help from powerful people. It took money, time, and organization. Small explosives brought the plaza down and the ship with it and then large explosives finally did enough damage to destroy a gossamer ship.

Just one of many ships, but it said something to the aliens. They left. Without a word. Without retaliating. Without helping us.

And we learned something about the alien themselves, or rather we learned that we knew less than we thought. The tall, spindly gossamer beings at the signing disappeared when the explosion occurred. They just disappeared. The aliens, whatever they looked like, hadn't left the ship. The gossamer beings had just been their avatars.

On the personal front, Grace and I were communicating regularly now via Facebook. Tracy was in hospice, they had caught the cancer late, and she didn't have long. Not at all.

I couldn't call it a silver lining or anything. The world at large was going to shit and the only woman I ever truly loved was dying. But I was grateful to at least be able to exchange messages with my only daughter.

"Happy Fourth!" Walt Green said with a grin on his face. This was the guy that looked kind of like me and drew my attention to the screen so I saw the explosion when it happened. He had on shorts and a T-shirt that was a wraparound American flag.

The dummy was happy about it all. He became a regular, like the bar was somehow the magic that had made the reality he wanted come to pass.

"Happy Fourth," I echoed without the enthusiasm. He had said this to me every time he had come to get a beer. Above me on the screen was coverage of the celebration, fireworks going off in Los Angeles. I pulled him another pint and added it to his tab.

I watched him go and he was so happy. I wished I could be, but we still had the same damn problems we had before the aliens came and we weren't making a bit of progress on any of it. Politicians fought, the talking heads on the news talked about it endlessly, and nothing changed.

But it was a large crowd and the beer was flowing and the receipts would be good. I shrugged and tried to shake it off when I heard shouting outside up on the street.

It wasn't one shout, but many, and the timbre of it was more surprise than fear, but something was going on.

"...we are getting report of...well, something falling from the sky," the silver-haired anchor was saying from the screen. While much of the bar emptied out and hustled up the stairs to see what it was, I turned to the screen.

The view changed, away from the fireworks over LA, and I could see it. Shimmering threads falling from the sky, all silvery and bright, like Christmas tinsel.

The camera was shaking but it zoomed in. The tinsel-like threads glimmered and twisted as they fell from the sky, seemingly everywhere at once.

"This is not a local phenomenon," the anchor said. "This is happening worldwide. The color of the threads, well...I can only say they appear to be...gossamer."

I froze. That color was forever associated with the aliens. Was this them? Was this their retaliation? The shouting outside became louder and a bit schizophrenic. Some sounded happy, delighted, like a child would be at seeing such a wonder. Other voices sounded fearful.

The bar began to refill as those that feared what was coming headed for shelter.

I was rooted in place watching the scene on TV. The talking heads talked, but I wasn't really listening anymore.

The threads, the gossamer threads, were from the aliens. They had to be. As the minutes slipped by, I was like the crowd outside, sometimes fearful, sometimes hopeful.

The screen showed the threads twisting and falling and as their scale became clear I could see that they were each about two feet long and thin. And they were everywhere. There must be billions of them, maybe more, maybe a lot more.

Flagstaff is up at 7,000 feet in elevation, so the threads hit here first, before they did on TV. They fell and hit the building above me and kept falling floor after floor until they came through the roof of the bar.

People screamed. People cowered. I just stood there and held my hand out.

I still had hope.

I was a fool.

The thread felt cool when it touched me and a tingle passed through my body, which seemed to absorb the thread, and then...it seemed like it was over.

But it wasn't.

"YOU OKAY?" I SENT to Grace on Facebook from my phone. I had broken down and installed it since Grace was actually communicating. "Did one of those threads contact you?"

The bar was hopping, people asking for shots, but I had excused myself to the bathroom.

"Yeah," she wrote back. "One got Mom too. She woke up for a minute and told me she was dreaming about our trip Roosevelt Lake when I was six. She seemed happy."

The bathroom stunk of too many poorly aimed streams like it always did, but I smiled. That was a long reply for Grace.

That was the summer I bought us a boat and thought I knew everything there was to know by doing a little research on the Internet.

"Calling for help was soooo embarrassing," I wrote. I ran us out of gas, not realizing the boat had a backup tank and all I needed to do was flip a switch.

"You are occasionally stupid in the most adorable way," she wrote back.

I stared at it. I needed to be careful. The connection was tenuous, but it was strengthening.

"Thank you," I typed. "You are always adorable."

I got a smiley emoji out of her and she told me she had to go.

SOME SAID THE GOSSAMER threads were a hoax, that nothing had happened, that the aliens were even more impotent than we thought. Others hoped that the aliens had taken pity on us, that the gossamer threads were alien tech and would start capturing carbon, would help us stop this pending crisis.

I didn't believe either.

The aliens wouldn't have drooped trillions of them around the globe at the same time as a hoax. And as far as it being carbon-gobbling tech, that made no sense. We humans could do something ourselves about the crisis be we lacked the collective will. That had been the most powerful part of the Treaty. Bringing us together as a world.

But no aliens, no treaty, same old human race.

But soon the whispers started. People talked about seeing ghosts of the recently dead.

Thursday afternoon I was home, in my small house back against the ponderosa pine tree forest in a little development south of Flagstaff. Summer was all about fire danger and I was late in getting my pine needles cleaned up.

We had had some bad fires lately and this one little thing, cleaning up pine needles, most folks had gotten serious about. The threat was close enough and real enough for us to actually do something about it.

Walt Green, my alien-hating customer, turned out to be a neighbor. He had moved into the community recently and we were... well, I can't say we were becoming friends. We would have a beer every once in a while and he would go on about the aliens like I agreed with him.

I had opinions. I was just not used to expressing them. Could be one of the reasons I'm not married anymore. You've got to communicate in a marriage.

Anyway, I was raking up pine needles the afternoon after the gossamer threads fell, chewing it over in my mind, when Walt Green came running up, his face red and he was out of breath.

He still had on his wraparound flag T-shirt and he was huffing and puffing. Walt worked construction, was strong but with a bulging belly, and he was most definitely not the running type.

"Hide me, Glenn," he said, his eyes wide and darting around as if something horrible might be hiding behind each tree.

"Well hello to you too, Walt," I said, pausing in my raking. "What's going on?" The guy had a weird sense of humor and I thought this was one of his awkwardly strange pranks.

"She...I..." His eyes darted around more. "She is coming after me. She blames me."

His fear infected me and I started looking around. This was no joke. I grabbed him and pulled him to the deck on the back of my house, out of sight of the road.

"You're not making sense, Walt," I said. "Slow down. Tell me what happened."

"Shelia," he said, his breath coming in gasps and smelling sour. "She...she's dead. She...." He began to quietly sob. He was drunk when the bar closed and judging from his rumpled clothing, his potent halitosis, and his general state, he didn't stop drinking then.

I searched my mind. I learn a lot of names at the bar. An image popped into my head of a blond woman about our age who liked to wear a cowboy hat. She was a regular and I had seen her and Walt getting to know each other. They had left together last night.

I let go of him and stepped back. "Shelia is dead?" I asked.

His eyes widened and looked haunted. "The train...the train...the train..." he intoned. He wasn't right. He wasn't all here.

It happens nearly every year. The tracks run right through Flagstaff just across Route 66 from the bar. Someone gets in front of one. It is a gruesome reality.

And I could see it. Two drunk people stumbling out of my bar, making it across the road, standing there waiting for the freight train to pass and someone getting the bright idea to see how close they can get to the speeding train.

With CNN on so much at the bar, I have a no-news policy at home. I hadn't heard.

I sat down on one of the metal chairs. It scraped loudly against the worn wood of the deck.

I didn't know Shelia, not really. Just in the surface way a bartender gets to know their customers. Shelia always with her cowboy hat and loud laugh, she liked red wine and chicken wings, usually brought friends, often on a bar crawl and acting much younger than she was.

"What did you do, Walt?" I asked.

I'm not proud of that moment. It was way too easy for me to blame Walt, to assume he did something wrong. Just because we saw the world differently.

"Nothing," he hissed, looking around. "I told her to wait for the damn train, to not cross with the gates down and the lights flashing." His face darkened and he looked like we was far way. "She got her boot heel stuck in the track and…" His hands shook and his mouth quivered. "There was nothing I could do."

But that was not what he was thinking. I could see it on his face. He was thinking that he should have rushed to her aid, pulled her out of her boot and away from danger, but he was too drunk to walk straight much less run.

I don't know if Walt could read the expression on my face, but it said that I had played my part, taking their money and letting them both get good and drunk. Something I did every night that I worked.

———

TRACY, GRACE, AND I used to be a tribe of three. A single unit that worked together, that had each other's back. We were a family.

We would fight, we had our differences of course, but whenever the world pressed against us, we would unite and act as one.

As a team, we each had our roles. I would go off and help manage employees for the faceless megacorp. Tracy was an assistant teacher and kept the household running. Grace went to school and painted, which she showed a talent for at a young age.

I thought I was doing enough by funding most of our lifestyle. I thought that was my role. I worked long hours and I would need to withdraw when I came home. I'm not saying I ignored my family, that I didn't go to recitals or help around the house. I did. It's just that my work left so little left of m e.

And eventually Tracy had enough. She wanted more. She went out and found it in a teacher at her school named Trent.

I remember the night that our tribe fractured and I was ejected from it. Our big Scottsdale home was empty, too empty. All tiled floors and vaulted ceilings, but no Grace, no Tracy. It was almost seven p.m. when I came home, kind of a normal workday for me.

"Hello," I said, feeling the emptiness. "Anyone home?"

The plush living room was empty, the kitchen sparkling clean, no dinner on the mahogany dining room table.

I wandered through the house until I found Tracy in our bedroom. She had a suitcase packed but still open. In it was my clothing. She sat in the rocking chair by the bay window slowly rocking back and forth.

"Grace is starting college in the fall," she said, her voice steady. Her black hair was freshly washed, hanging damp against her neck, her favorite pink robe wrapped around her thin body. "I can finally do this."

She laid it all out. The affair. How her and Trent had plans to get married. How horrified she was that I hadn't figured it out. How this was the end of our family.

I was relieved. Honestly. I was mad and sad and felt used, all those other emotions. But I was relieved. I hated my job. I hated the hours. And if I wasn't working for this family, to keep it all going, then I wasn't going to work like that anymore.

Two months later I was in Flagstaff helping to renovate the bar, trying to build a new life.

GHOSTS. THAT WAS WHAT the aliens gifted us with. Ghosts.

It took time for understanding, but it didn't take long for everyone to know something was happening. Something terrible.

I thought Walt was imagining things. I brought him inside. I gave him a shot of whiskey, the good stuff. I tried to calm him down.

He sat there on my worn couch, hunched over and sobbing. Saying things that didn't
make sense.

"The...the body," he began after downing the whiskey. "Not much left but the ghost... It was standing there. It was staring at me. It was her. Glowing silver. In her cowboy boots and hat."

I stared at him, my jaw open. I stood on the old hardwood floor of my place. I wanted to pace. I wanted to get back out into the sun, but I couldn't move.

He raised his head, his bloodshot eyes meeting mine. "She talked to me, Glenn. I couldn't hear her, but her mouth was moving. She said the same thing over and over so many times I could read her lips. 'You did this,' that's what she said."

I still couldn't speak but he must have read the look on my face.

"I'm not crazy," he said, licking his lips and eyeing the bottle of whiskey I had in my hand. I poured him another couple of fingers and he shot it back. "She'll be here. Any minute. And then you'll know." He blinked rapidly, way too many times. "I keep running from her. I keep hiding, but..." He swallowed hard. "She always finds me."

———

TRACY AND TRENT DIDN'T last. Nor the two men after that. And this made me feel good and feel bad.

My ego loved it. She had made it sound like the split was all about me, all about me not being available, and I was glad it wasn't all about me. And I felt bad for such petty thoughts.

But our little tribe, our little family unit, there was no getting that back together.

"Grace, you need to be careful," I messaged, while Walt mumbled on my couch, not really even aware of me anymore.

My stomach was in knots as I kept an eye on Walt as he drank more whiskey and mumbled to himself. My eyes kept looking out the picture windows at the forest, worried that something was coming.

Tracy had gotten Grace in the divorce. She was an adult, just an adult, when it happened. I was the bad guy, they bonded over it, they were closer than they had been since she was a girl.

Another reason I fled to Flagstaff. "Why?" Grace messaged back.

"The threads. Something's going on." I wasn't believing Walt. Not yet. But I was believing that things weren't right. And I needed to reach out to my daughter even if I didn't understand what was going on.

"How is your mother?" I sent when her reply didn't come back.

"Not long now," she replied and a cold sweat broke out on my neck.

"Be careful," I sent again.

I DON'T DRINK WHEN I'm on duty and taking care of Walt felt like it was duty.

Twenty minutes later when Walt's continuing babble was starting to wear me down and I needed a drink, the ghost of Shelia Newberry walked in.

That feeling I had in February when the alien's ship was blown up, that we were all screwed, was no longer a feeling. I knew it. I was looking at it.

She looked just like she had last night, dressed in tight jeans, a low-cut blouse, and her ever-present cowboy boots and hat. Except she looked like she was made out of moonlight, out of gossamer.

My living room has lots of windows facing the forest so she was a bit hard to see in the light, but there was no denying it. It was Shelia. She was a ghost.

And she was mad.

Shelia was always pretty fiery and that was on display here. She was pointing at Walt, her outstretched, long-nailed finger shaking as she yelled at him.

You did this.

Even though I couldn't hear her, I could see her lips form that phrase over and over.

Walt ran away, like the devil himself was on his tail, and the ghost of Shelia Newberry slowly walked after him.

THE NEXT DAY I couldn't really function and sat on the couch staring out my big picture windows at the forest.

Shelia Green was a ghost. I watched some of the news and reports of ghosts such as her were rampant. The talking heads thought it was the aliens.

Gossamer aliens, gossamer threads, gossamer ghosts.

The mechanism involved was anyone's guess. Some kind of tech so unfathomable to us, but if they were right, those threads invaded us, knew us, became a version of us when we died.

The religious were shitting themselves, talking of Judgement Day. Some of them thought the aliens were a manifestation of the devil and the ghosts where here to test us. Others thought that it was God's gift, these vengeful ghosts, to keep us on the righteous path. And a few thought that the ghosts were the souls of the dead risen like Jesus before them.

I didn't know what to think, so I sat there and stared.

Grace wasn't returning my messages anymore and I hadn't gotten much sleep. I worried that Tracy had died, that Tracy was haunting Grace and she would soon be as desperate as Walt.

So I sat and I stared at the forest. It's kind of why I moved up here. The forest is still, it is constant, it is steady. Even when I'm not. Especially when I'm not.

A banging on the door startled me back to myself and I got up and opened it. Walt was standing there, still in the same clothing, his face unshaved, his hair unkempt, and his complexion sallow.

"I can't sleep," he said. "She won't let me sleep."

The ghost of Shelia Newbury wasn't here yet, but I knew it wouldn't be long. It was clear now how these ghosts worked. Shelia blamed Walt for her death so her ghost haunted him, her gossamer ghost.

No religion required. This was the simple logic of the aliens.

Actually, I don't know if it was simple for them, but it was logical. I think they felt a need to teach humanity a lesson, so they rained their gossamer threads down on us, no one escaped them, and now when someone dies, if they feel someone else is at fault, they haunt them.

Forever.

I poured him a glass full of whiskey and he took a gulp of it. "I relive it, in my dreams," he said, not making any sense.

He was back on the couch and I was pacing this time. I had been doing a lot of pacing when I wasn't zoned out and staring. "What do you relive, Walt?"

"That moment," he said, gulping more whiskey. "When...when she was on the tracks, when she felt the rumble of the train below her feet, when her boot got stuck, when the light shined in her eyes and then she looked to me, when..." He trailed off, gasping as if he had just lived what he had described.

"You're reliving her death?" I asked.

He nodded, downing more whiskey. "From her eyes...feeling it all...like it's goddamn real...including her blame of me."

I stood there blinking, my jaw moving, but I didn't know what to say. The news hadn't said anything about this.

The gossamer ghosts did more than just haunt who they blamed, they revisited their deaths on them, whenever they slept.

Walt stayed until the ghost of Shelia Newbury came and then he ran off whimpering.

I flopped back down on the couch, worried about Grace, worried for this world.

———

"Mom's gone," Grace messaged me, startling me from my stupor. The day had slid into late afternoon and I had hardly moved from the couch. I had heard noises, cars driving by, shouts, but I couldn't rouse myself to do anything. The house had gotten warm in the summer day and I hadn't even got up to open the windows.

I stared at my phone and swallowed hard. I didn't type anything because I knew there was more. There had to be more.

"She's one of those things," she messaged.

"Where is she now?" I typed, my hands shaking.

"She left."

My breath whooshed out of me in relief.

Tracy wasn't haunting Grace.

"Can you come?" she messaged. "Can you help me, Dad?"

I just stared at the phone, blinking. Grace hadn't asked me for anything in years but the thought of going to Phoenix, a big city where many people die every day, where there were gossamer ghosts roaming, was terrifying.

"Of course," I messaged back.

———

As I drove into the desert sprawl of Phoenix, Arizona, I could almost believe that nothing had happened. The streets were dense with cars, the heat reaching 105 outside, the sky dusty and hazy, all of it looking rather otherworldly after being in Flagstaff amongst the trees.

I didn't listen to the news on the way down, just blasted classic rock and tried not to think about what had happened.

We blew up the alien's ship, they rained their threads down on us, and the word was fracturing, soon to be crumbling.

I thought it would be climate change that would put a dent in humanity, not weird karmic ghosts driven by alien tech.

I drove to the address Grace had texted me. I was a little surprised when I realized it was a park, Encato Park, a sprawling expanse with green grass and palm trees, shallow lakes, even a little amusement park.

The heat was like a blowtorch when I got out of the car and looked around. I heard the slap, slap of a basketball from a nearby court and the sounds of children playing in the distance.

It was a strange moment. It felt normal, but I didn't trust it.

"I'm here," I messaged Grace, "at the parking lot."

"Wait there," she messaged back almost immediately.

I moved to the edge of the lot, letting the scant shade of one of the park's trees shield me from the sun.

I saw Grace first. She looked tired, her blond hair pulled back into a tight ponytail dressed in tan shorts and a loose white T-shirt. Not her usual stylish choice. She was signing like someone was with her, but I didn't see anyone.

Grace was born deaf. She was very shy, especially as a child, preferring her paints to being around people who didn't know how to sign.

I stepped forward and waved, doing my best to smile. I was sweating from the heat, much less used to it than I had been, and my stomach was rioting.

Something was going on beyond Tracy's death.

My estrangement from my daughter was a quiet one. A gradual distancing after Tracy and I split until I hardly knew her anymore. Her shyness and my shame combining to create ever-widening distance.

Grace stopped when she saw me and signed to the air next to her. She was close enough so I could read it. "It will be okay. He will at least listen to what you have to say."

My heart thumped in my chest and I squinted and saw a shimmering in the air next to Grace. It was hard to see in the harsh sunlight but Grace was talking to a gossamer ghost.

And that ghost had to be Tracy.

I almost ran. Did Tracy blame me for her death and just couldn't find me like Shelia always seemed to find Walt?

But this was my daughter and she had reached out.

They moved into the shade of a tree and I could see the ghost more clearly. I rubbed my sweaty palms on my shorts and stepped forward, signing, "Hello, Grace. It is so good to see you." I then signed to the ghost, "I am so sorry for what happened to you, Tracy."

The ghost still looked like Tracy with her shoulder-length hair and her generous curves, except she was gossamer, looking like she was made out of light. She was dressed in a sweats, the same thing she was wearing when she died.

"Can I come with you?" Tracy signed, a shy smile on her face. Her weight looked good and I had to imagine it wasn't like that when she died.

"What?" I signed. "You don't blame me for your death, do you?" My heart was pounding and the heat was making me lightheaded. "No. Of course not," she signed, and then silvery tears formed in her eyes and she looked away. "I made a mistake, Glenn, and I miss you."

Tracy was what we would soon come to know as a wandering ghost. They don't blame anyone for their death but they are still looking for their place, looking for someone to take them in.

"Please," Grace signed. "She..." Her face clouded and I could see the tears she was holding back. "She is still so much Mom. This is what she wants."

I would have said no but for Grace.

I DIDN'T GET ENOUGH time with Grace. I was starving for it but she told me she had missed too much school and had to get back, rushing off leaving me there with the ghost of my dead wife.

The trip up from the valley was quiet and strange, the silvery glow sitting there always visible out of the corner of my eye. When Tracy talked, I couldn't hear her, just like Shelia Newbury and the rest of the ghosts. And I couldn't sign to her while I was driving, but every time I glanced, she smiled at me shyly and my heart fluttered in my chest.

I had always been the shy one, more comfortable with work than intimacy.

I kept telling myself that this wasn't Tracy. Tracy was dead. This was some bizarre alien tech, the result of the gossamer threads. But it felt like Tracy and I liked how that felt.

When we got to the house and the cooler, pine-tree-scented air of Flagstaff, I walked in and she stayed standing at the threshold.

"What are you waiting for?" I signed.

The sun had set and I could see her a lot more clearly. She blinked and her brow furrowed. "I think you need to invite me in."

I stared at her and the moment drew out. I had seen Shelia Newbury go everywhere to get to Walt Green. But Tracy couldn't come in my house without my invitation like some kind of vampire?

I could just go to bed and leave here there. Maybe she would leave and I wouldn't have to spend the rest of my days with the gossamer ghost of my ex-wife.

But I didn't want that. "Please come in," I signed, and Tracy smiled, walking into my house.

We talked, late into the night, and when I sleep, I dreamed of Tracy's death. I felt her pain, heavily muffled by drugs. I felt her fear. I heard Grace weeping quietly as Tracy slipped from consciousness.

Just like Walt experienced Shelia's death, I was experiencing Tracy's. Another aspect of these gossamer ghosts.

———

I AM NOT ALONE anymore.

It's a strange thing and I am having trouble getting used to it, but Tracy's ghost didn't want to haunt me, not in the normal sense of the word as we are coming to understand it. She just wanted to be with me.

As had Tracy when she was still alive. After she got sick, she had wanted to heal our divide but didn't know how to, so now her gossamer ghost was carrying that mission out.

The ghost and I have an advantage over most people dealing with these alien constructs. We both sign. We can easily communicate. Well, I don't need to sign, she can hear me, it's me that can't hear her. But I sign most of the time anyway, it just feels right.

It's not like she knows anything about the aliens, but she can tell me the things she is feeling, the things she wants. And it's pretty simple. She just wants to belong somewhere. She wants to have something to do.

In that way she is just like the rest of us, but for her it's out in the open, not buried under layers of ego and complicated psychology.

She's still Tracy, but she is, in many ways, much simpler than she used to be.

She never leaves the house. She now spends the night as far away from me as she can and still be in the house.

I dream of her death most every night but it wasn't a horrible death. I think maybe it's not all bad. I know what it feels like to die, and while it is not comfortable, it's not actually foreign to me anymore.

We talk when I get home from the bar, her silvery hands signing brightly as I sit on the couch with only a single lamp on so I can really see her.

She's filling me in on the years we've been apart, on the years I missed with Grace. She asks me about my day and listens. She seems a little sad but content.

We watch the news together, watch what is happening in the world. Suicide rates are skyrocketing. Wars are ending. Some are abandoning their jobs. People are becoming a lot more careful in how they move through this world. They don't want a gossamer ghost haunting them.

Two weeks later, when I came home, Tracy asked me how my day was. Which was normal, but then she really looked at my face. "Are you all right, Glenn?" she signed.

I shook my head. "Walt Green is dead," I signed. I had told her about my experience of the gossamer threads of Walt and Shelia.

She stood there blinking, clearly unsure of what to say, which was pure Tracy. She felt deeply but always had trouble with the words.

"He jumped off the building the bar is in," I signed. "Shelia was up there on the roof, it looked like she was yelling at him. Guess two weeks of it was just too much."

I paused, the sight and sound of it still haunting me. I could hear his body striking the ground, his bones breaking.

"He's a ghost now, of course," I continued, "and he's haunting Shelia Newbury. They walked off together looking like they were screaming at each other."

A ghost haunting a ghost. Yelling at each other, blaming each other for as long as they exist. It was a chilling thought, and then again, somehow not that surprising. We humans can hold grudges and now our ghosts do too.

Tracy couldn't take my hand. She couldn't hold me. But whatever this gossamer ghost was, she was made up of the woman I had loved for so many years. She had the same mannerism and knew the same things.

It wasn't everything I wanted, but in some strange way the aliens brought Tracy back to me.

"Do you want to talk about it?" she signed.

I shrugged my shoulders. "Can we just watch the news?"

She smiled, it was a sad, compassionate smile and we sat on the couch together and watch the world unravel a little at a time.

I don't know what is coming. Some people think we'll hold it together, that this will make us better people, but the signs of everything falling apart are hard not to see.

Grace messages all the time now. To talk to me and the ghost of her mother. She wants to come up and visit soon.

I don't know what the aliens were thinking with their gossamer threads. How can I know. Was it punishment? Are they trying to teach us a lesson? Is there more to come?

As the talking heads babbled on the TV, I glanced over at Tracy. She was chewing on her thumbnail even though she doesn't have a thumb.

The world was falling apart, but I kinda, sorta, almost had my family back.

More Sci-fi?

Want more sci-fi? Check out *Seeing Forever*, a novel about love and loss in a post-biological existence.

A Life Worth Living

Paul Cruz is no longer human. He's a Singular, his consciousness technological, no longer biological. He was there at the beginning and helped ensure the survival of all the Singulars. Free from the limits of flesh and blood, he wanted to live forever, but now that he's lost what he cares about the most, forever is too long, much too long.

After suspending himself for decades, he is about to enter a virtual world called "Home" to take one last look around. But Home is not what he expected and what he finds will change everything.

When is forever too long?

Get Seeing Forever now or find out more at RobertJMc-Carter.com/books/SeeingForever

About the Author

Robert J. McCarter is the author of more than ten novels and over a hundred short stories. He is a regular contributor to *Pulphouse Fiction Magazine* and his short fiction has also appeared in *The Saturday Evening Post*, *Andromeda Spaceways Inflight Magazine*, *Everyday Fiction*, and numerous anthologies.

Robert writes in a variety of genres from contemporary fantasy to science fiction and just about everything in between. His diverse background–including a career in software engineering, growing up on a ranch riding horses, and acting–colors the stories he tells.

He lives in the mountains of Arizona with his amazing wife and his ridiculously adorable dogs.

Find out more at RobertJMcCarter.com

Books by Robert J. McCarter

Short Stores Collections

Life After: Stories of Life, Death, and the Places in Between

Anomalous Readings: Thirteen Curious and Confounding Tales

Creatures Featured: Thirteen Stories of Monsters and other Creatures

Selected Novels

Seeing Forever

Where the Past Belongs: An Angelica and Ash Time Travel Adventure

Series

The Woody and June versus the Apocalypse: WoodyAndJune.com
A Ghost's Memoir: ShuffledOff.com
Neutrinoman and Lightningirl: A Love Story: Neutrinoman.com

Carterville Mysteries: CartervilleAz.com
Conner Bright Mysteries: RobertJMcCarter.com/series/ConnerBright
Hollow Earth: RobertJMcCarter.com/series/HollowEarth

For more information, go to RobertJMcCarter.com

www.ingramcontent.com/pod-product-compliance
Lightning Source LLC
Chambersburg PA
CBHW020322150626
46552CB00022B/3152